Walt Disney's
Sleeping Beauty

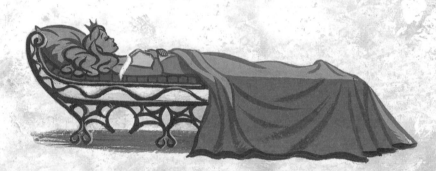

Illustrations by The Walt Disney Studios

Story adapted by Monique Peterson
Illustrations adapted by Norm McGary

Reader's Digest
Children's Books™

Pleasantville, New York • Montréal, Québec • Bath, United Kingdom

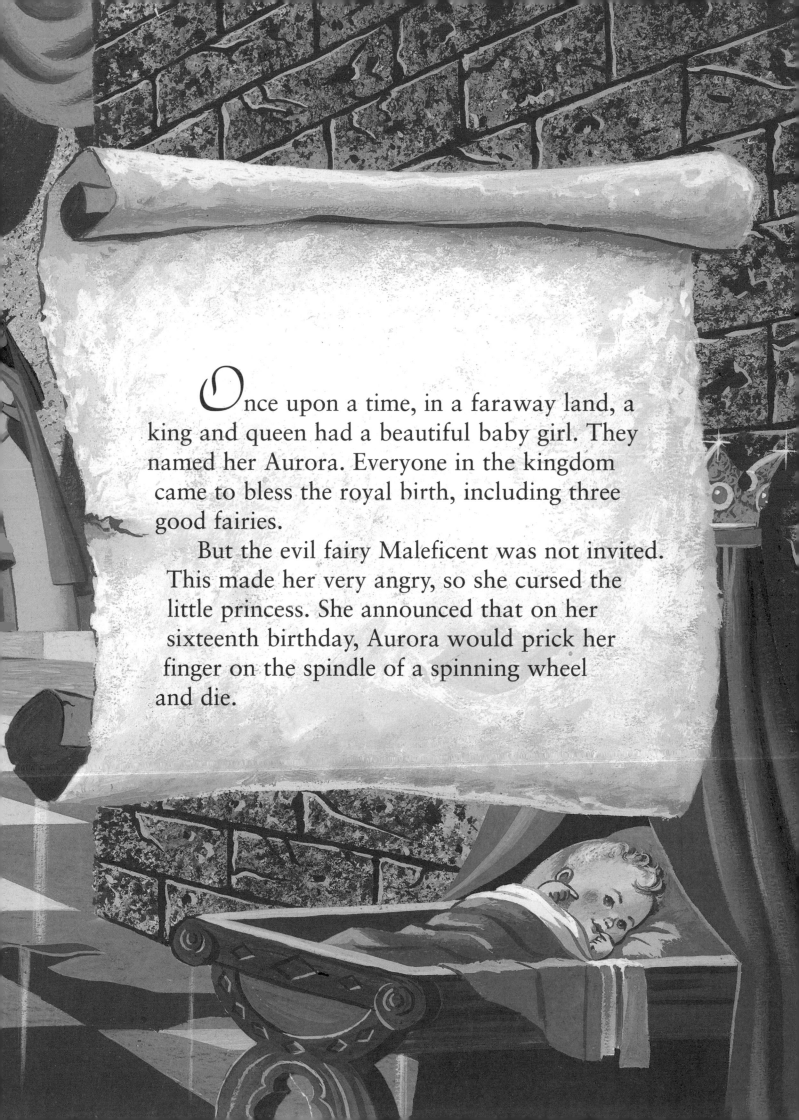

Once upon a time, in a faraway land, a king and queen had a beautiful baby girl. They named her Aurora. Everyone in the kingdom came to bless the royal birth, including three good fairies.

But the evil fairy Maleficent was not invited. This made her very angry, so she cursed the little princess. She announced that on her sixteenth birthday, Aurora would prick her finger on the spindle of a spinning wheel and die.

The king and queen were horrified. But the good fairies, Flora, Fauna, and Merryweather, came up with a plan to protect Princess Aurora from Maleficent.

They disguised themselves as peasants and raised Aurora deep in the woods. To be extra safe, the fairies agreed to stop using magic so that no one — especially Maleficent — would be suspicious.

Sixteen years went by, and no one discovered Aurora's secret home. Her only companions were the birds and fluffy-tailed squirrels and rabbits.

But the princess was never lonely, for she played with her
animal friends every day. She sang to them, and told them
about her dreams of falling in love.

On Princess Aurora's sixteenth birthday, her dreams came true! Prince Phillip heard a beautiful song in the forest and followed the sound. He came upon a clearing and found Aurora, singing. They fell in love at first sight. All Aurora's forest friends shared in their joy as the happy couple danced and danced.

Meanwhile, the fairies were planning a secret birthday surprise for Aurora. Fauna tried to whip up a fancy layer cake. She opened a recipe book and started mixing all the ingredients in a big bowl.

Flora wanted to make Aurora an extra special dress. She used Merryweather as a model. First, Flora cut a hole in the center of the cloth for Aurora's head to fit through!

Poor Fauna didn't know the first thing about making a cake. She tried and tried and tried, but the only thing she could make was a gooey mess.

And Flora had never made a dress before. She snipped and clipped here and pinned and patched there, but she only succeeded in making Merryweather cry. Flora had stitched together a gown absolutely unfit for a princess.

Merryweather finally had enough of Flora and Fauna's nonsense. After sixteen years, it was time to get out their wands. They needed magic to clean up their mess! So, with a few simple whisks of their wands . . . Fauna's cake rose to perfection with pink icing and brilliant candles.

And Flora's fabric gathered itself, trimmed itself, and sewed itself together. With a wave of her wand, it became a lovely pink gown. Oh, no, thought Merryweather, that won't do. And in the blink of an eye, she changed the gown's color to a brilliant blue.

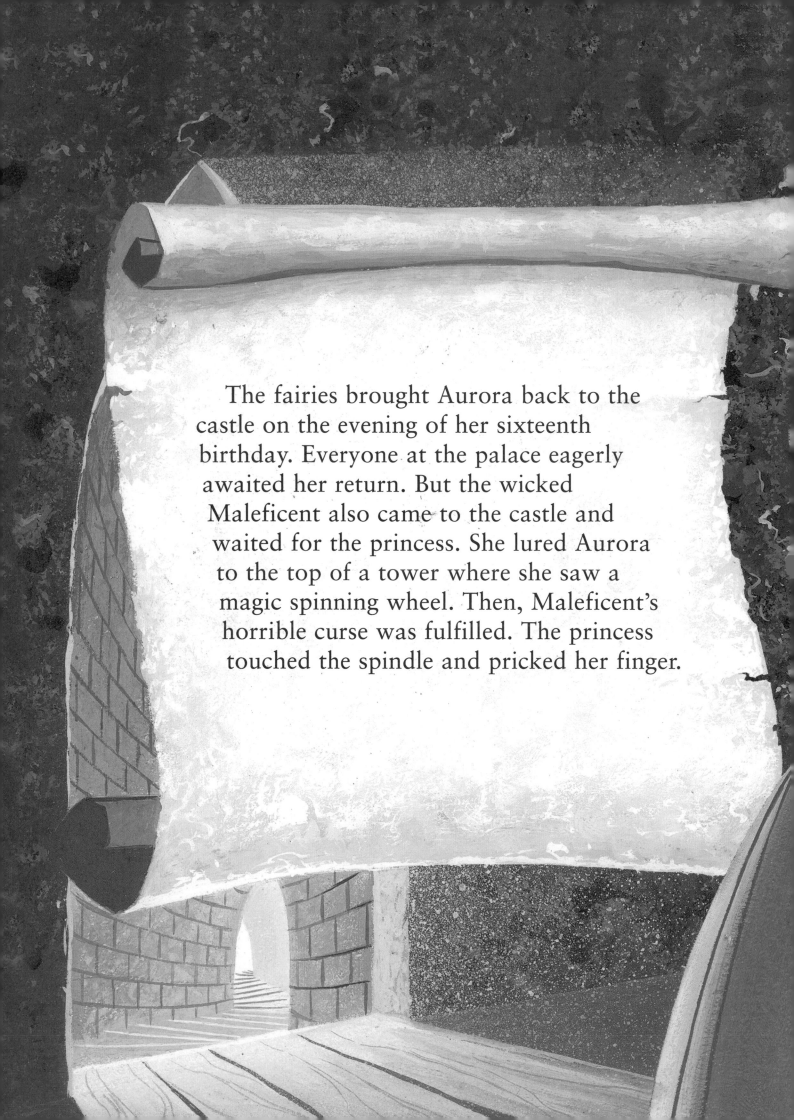

The fairies brought Aurora back to the castle on the evening of her sixteenth birthday. Everyone at the palace eagerly awaited her return. But the wicked Maleficent also came to the castle and waited for the princess. She lured Aurora to the top of a tower where she saw a magic spinning wheel. Then, Maleficent's horrible curse was fulfilled. The princess touched the spindle and pricked her finger.

The princess fell to the floor. The fairies wept, for they couldn't stop Maleficent. But Aurora didn't die. The good fairies had worked their magic so that the princess simply fell into a deep sleep. She would awaken only after the first kiss from her true love.

Flora, Fauna, and Merryweather couldn't bear to break
the king's heart with the news of Aurora's fate. So they made
everyone else in the castle fall asleep, too — all the guards, the
ladies-in-waiting, even the king and queen.

Once the palace was totally quiet, the fairies flew away with magical speed. They needed to find the handsome prince who would break the spell.

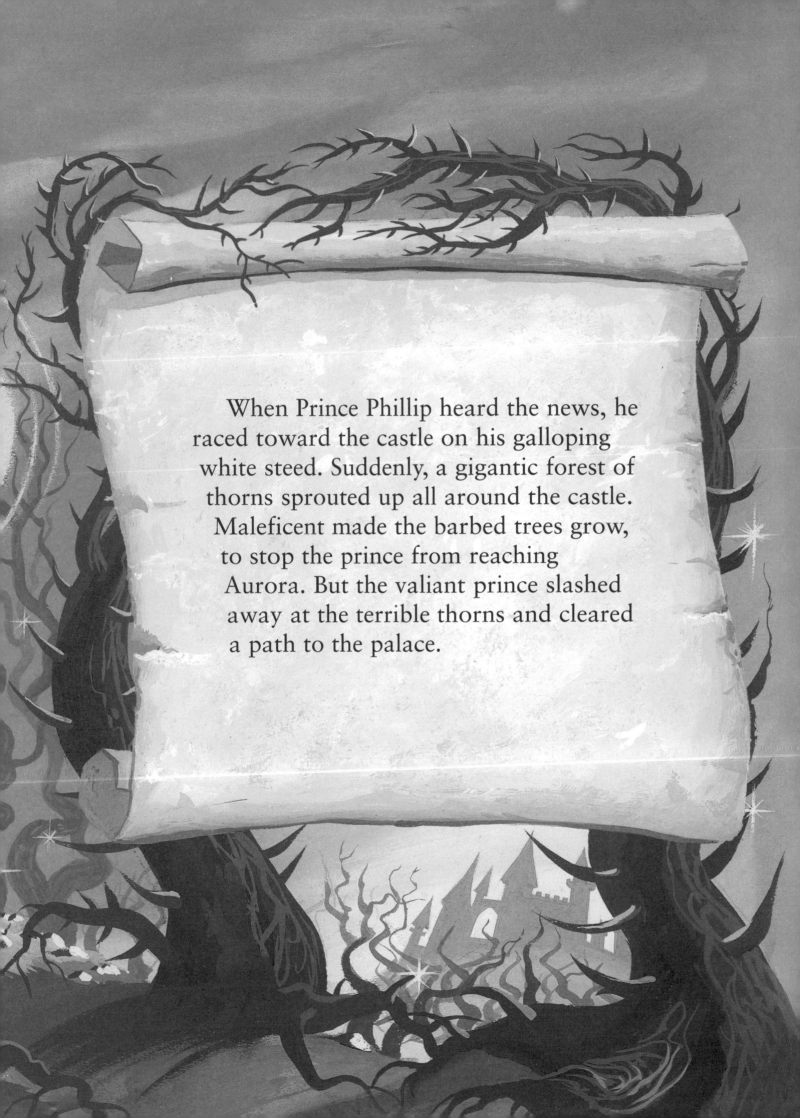

When Prince Phillip heard the news, he raced toward the castle on his galloping white steed. Suddenly, a gigantic forest of thorns sprouted up all around the castle. Maleficent made the barbed trees grow, to stop the prince from reaching Aurora. But the valiant prince slashed away at the terrible thorns and cleared a path to the palace.

As soon as the prince got to the palace, a fierce and furious dragon appeared before him. It was Maleficent, who used all her powers to transform herself into a fire-breathing dragon! The dragon blasted Phillip with a fierce blaze.

The prince stumbled back and nearly fell off a cliff. But using all his strength, he held up his shield and hurled his mighty sword deep into the heart of the dragon. The monstrous Maleficent was slain, once and for all!

The prince dashed to Aurora's side and gave her a kiss. The princess began to stir. Her eyelids fluttered open, and she awoke at last! Happiness filled her heart when she saw her handsome prince.

Then, the fairies' spell lifted, as one by one, the king and queen and everyone else awoke from their slumber, yawning and stretching.

Soon, the palace was buzzing with
news of Princess Aurora and Prince Phillip.
The king and queen ordered a royal feast
in the royal banquet hall. And the festivities
continued in the magnificent ballroom,
where everyone made merry with music
and dancing and laughter. The three
good fairies were most joyous of all,
for they knew Sleeping Beauty had
found true love. The prince and princess
danced the night away and lived happily
forevermore.